DORRIE and the WEATHER-BOX

by Patricia Coombs

LOTHROP, LEE & SHEPARD CO., INC.
New York

For Betsy, Andy and Richie

This is Dorrie. She is a witch. A little witch. Her room is mixed up, her socks are mixed up, and her hat is always on crooked. Her mother is the Big Witch.

One Wednesday Dorrie was looking in her closet for her other shoe and she found a picnic basket.

Dorrie looked at the picnic basket. She looked at her black cat, Gink.

"Gink," said Dorrie, "we need a picnic to go in the basket. Maybe Mother and Cook would like to have a picnic, too."

Down, down, down the stairs went Dorrie and Gink went with her.

Dorrie and Gink went into the kitchen. Cook was muttering and kneading bread dough and frowning very hard.

"Cook," said Dorrie, "where is Mother?"

Cook frowned harder and gave the bread dough another whack.

"We're all out of toadstools and she has gone to borrow some from Mr. Obs. They will be back later for tea. I'm busy making bread, so run and play."

"Oh," said Dorrie. "We're going on a picnic. Would you like to go on a picnic with Gink and me?"

Cook stopped whacking the bread and stamped her foot.

"A picnic! It's raining out. Go upstairs and play and don't ask silly questions. I'm busy!"

Dorrie took the picnic basket and went slowly up the stairs. Gink went with her.

"Gink," said Dorrie, "if the clouds went away the rain would stop. If the rain stopped we could go on a picnic."

Gink meowed.

"Shhh!" said Dorrie. "I'm busy thinking." She looked down the hall at the little door that led to the tower stairs. At the top of the stairs was the secret room where the Big Witch made magic.

Dorrie tiptoed over to the door. "Hmmm," said Dorrie. "Mother forgot and left the key in the door. I bet she was going to fix the weather before she left and didn't have time. Come on, Gink."

Dorrie opened the door and climbed up the dark stairs. Up and up and up she went and Gink went with her.

Dorrie opened the door to the secret room and went inside. It was dark and spooky and bats flew past her hat. Dorrie shut the door.

Dorrie got out the Big Witch's book of magic
and turned the pages.

But she couldn't find any recipes for melting clouds. There was a recipe for cleaning crystal balls, and one for emptying ponds and puddles and filling them up again.

"I bet if I mixed the two together," said Dorrie, "it would work for clouds."

Dorrie got out the bottles and jars and put them beside the cauldron.

"Now, Gink," said Dorrie, "I'll open the window so the clouds can come in here, and I'll find something big with a lid to keep them in."

Dorrie looked around. In a dark corner she saw a big box. She pulled it in front of the window and lifted the lid up.

"There," said Dorrie.

DANGER
WEATHER BOX

Dorrie began pouring stuff from the bottles and jars into the cauldron. She poured in yellow stuff, and pink stuff, and orange stuff. She dumped in black powder and white powder and stirred it around and around. It began to boil and bubble and glitter, and the smoke curled around and around the room and went out the window. The cauldron bubbled harder and harder.

Gink hid under the table beside the picnic basket.

Dorrie sang as she stirred:

"Abracadabra blinkety-blue
Cloud-wish, out-loud wish,
Wish-away, wish-away, do."

She sang it over and over and over.

The smoke got blacker and blacker and thicker and thicker. The little room got darker and darker.

"Oh my," said Dorrie. She sneezed. Gink sneezed.

The stuff in the cauldron bubbled slowly away.

"This is not a very good recipe," said Dorrie. "It smells awful. But maybe the clouds are going into the box. Let's look, Gink."

Suddenly there was a loud crash of thunder. There was a flash of pink lightning and a flash of yellow lightning. The lightning was shooting out of the box and zigzagging all around the room. The bats squeaked and flapped their wings. Thunder crashed again and the box shook.

"Oh, oh," said Dorrie. "Something is going wrong. That box is too small. The storm is coming out instead of going in."

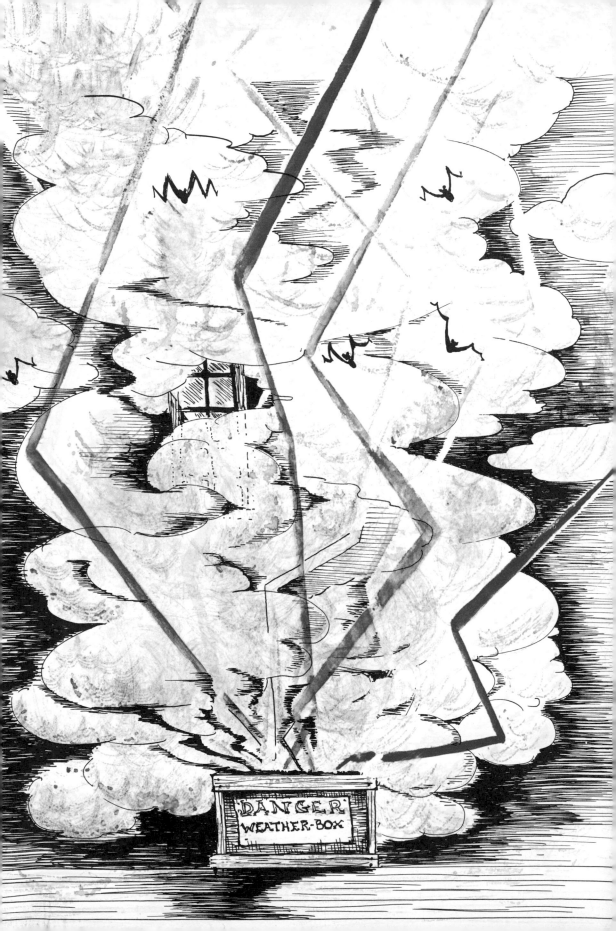

Dorrie tiptoed over to the box. She pushed the lid down, but it blew off and the lightning zigzagged everywhere. Thunder shook the room and knocked the bottles of magic all over the floor.

Dorrie and Gink ran out of the little room and slammed the door.

Down, down, down the stairs they ran and into the hall.

Dorrie slammed the door to the tower and
leaned against it.

"Oh, my," said Dorrie.

A black cloud came through a crack in the door. Orange lightning zigzagged through the keyhole.

The cloud grew bigger and bigger and blacker and blacker.

Dorrie put out her hand. It was raining.

"Oh, Gink," said Dorrie. "We've got the storm *inside* the house. We'll have to try to keep this door shut tight until it clears up."

Dorrie pushed a table and chairs against the door. It was raining harder and harder. Dorrie ran downstairs and got the umbrella and ran upstairs again.

She opened the umbrella and sat down in one of the chairs. Gink sat down beside her.

The clouds were getting thicker and thicker
and darker and darker. Rain splashed harder and
harder.

Dorrie heard someone shouting. Cook was
splashing around the hall, shouting and shaking
her fist at the clouds.

"Oh my," said Dorrie, "Cook is awfully cross."

There was a loud crash of thunder and Cook disappeared into the kitchen and slammed the door.

The blackest cloud of all swirled over Dorrie's head, and the wind started whistling through the hall. It blew harder and harder. It blew so hard that the tower door blew open and knocked over the chairs and table. Gink landed in the picnic basket.

"Sit tight, Gink," said Dorrie. The wind lifted them into the air and whirled them around and around and down the stairs.

They sailed into the parlor and out again.

Another gust of wind and a flash of lightning blew open the front door and they sailed right out the door.

Dorrie landed with a thump that knocked Gink out of the basket.

"Ooof," said Dorrie. She looked out from under the umbrella.

"Why, Gink," said Dorrie, "look! The sun is shining!"

There was a shadow beside her. Dorrie looked up. It was the Big Witch and Mr. Obs.

"Oh," said Dorrie. "I'm glad you're home, Mother. Hello, Mr. Obs."

"WHAT have you been doing?" said the Big Witch. "You're soaking wet! And the umbrella is torn and . . ."

A bolt of pink lightning shot out the front door and thunder shook the house.

The Big Witch looked into the hall. Mr. Obs looked, too.

"Amazing!" cried Mr. Obs. "An indoor storm, with pink and yellow and orange lightning. Just like Dorrie's socks."

The Big Witch frowned and looked at Dorrie.

"Dorrie," said the Big Witch. "What did you do while I was gone?"

Dorrie looked at the Big Witch. "I didn't do much of anything, Mother. I found the picnic basket, but it was raining outside so . . ."

"So," said the Big Witch, "you wanted to fix the weather. And as usual, you got into trouble. You not only mixed up my magic, you opened my weather box that says 'DO NOT OPEN.'"

Dorrie looked down at her toes. "I didn't know it was a weather box. It was just a funny box I was going to use to keep the clouds in. A storm came out of it instead."

"It certainly did!" cried Mr. Obs. "Look at the
tower!"

The tower was shaking and lightning was
shooting out of it in all directions.

The Big Witch grabbed the umbrella and sailed
into the house and disappeared up the stairs.

For a few minutes, Dorrie and Gink and Mr.
Obs looked through the front door.
Then slowly the lightning and thunder faded
away and the clouds changed color.

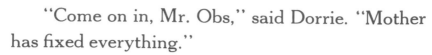

"Come on in, Mr. Obs," said Dorrie. "Mother has fixed everything."

They stood in the hall and looked at the clouds on the ceiling.

The Big Witch sailed down the stairs with the umbrella. "Now," she said, "that takes care of that . . ." She stopped and looked up. "Oh my," said the Big Witch. "Something went wrong!"

It was snowing. It was snowing orange snow, faster and faster and faster.

"I love snow!" cried Mr. Obs. "Nice, quiet, orange snow. Come on, Dorrie, we'll make a snow-man."

The Big Witch sailed back upstairs with the umbrella.

Dorrie and Mr. Obs made an orange snowman. It looked like Mr. Obs.

Suddenly the air grew brighter and brighter, and warmer and warmer. The snow stopped and the Big Witch came down the stairs.

The Big Witch looked around. "Dorrie," she said, "what did you do with Cook?"

"I don't think I turned her into anything," said Dorrie. "She must still be in the kitchen."

They all went into the kitchen. The oven door opened and Cook looked out. She yawned. "Is the storm over?" she said.

"Yes," said the Big Witch. "And it is time for tea."

Cook climbed out of the oven. She fixed tea and sandwiches and they all sat around the snowman in the hall and watched it melt.

When the snowman had nearly disappeared,
Mr. Obs took out his violin and played a tune.
Everybody clapped.

"Mother," said Dorrie, "I'm sorry I opened the lid of the weather box and mixed up the magic."

The Big Witch looked at Dorrie. "The next time you plan a picnic, don't try to change the weather. And now, go up to bed. Cook and I will mop up."

Dorrie said good night to the Big Witch, and to Mr. Obs, and to Cook, and climbed up, up, up the stairs. Gink went with her.

Dorrie put on her nightgown. She put the
picnic basket on the window sill and looked up at
the moon shining through the clouds.

"Gink," said Dorrie, "I wish . . . no, maybe I'd better not wish anything more until tomorrow. I'll just go to bed and dream I'm a Big Witch having a picnic on the moon."

Dorrie fell sound asleep

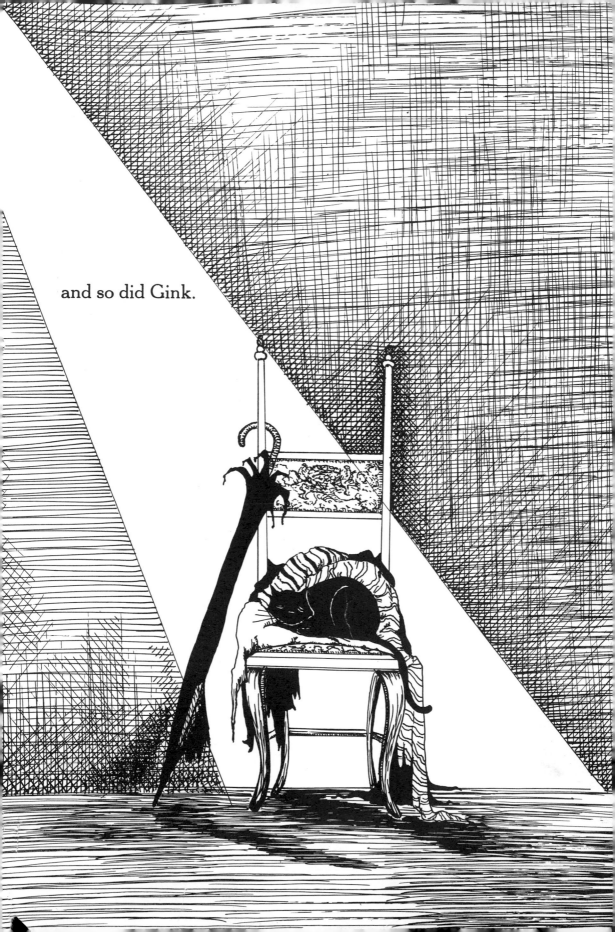

and so did Gink.